# GREEDY GRAHAM
by TONY GARTH

Graham was a very greedy little boy.

He spent every penny of his pocket money on sweets and sticky buns. And he never shared any of them with his friends.

He just gobbled them all up by himself.

At meal times, Graham's Mum, Dad and little brother, Malcolm, raced to get to the table before Graham. Otherwise there was no food left for them. Graham had eaten it all up.

However much he ate, Graham was never full. He always took a snack to bed with him in case he was hungry during the night.

At Malcolm's birthday party, Graham sneaked off while the others were playing pass-the-parcel and ate every last spoonful of jelly and ice cream. Not to mention every last crumb of Malcolm's birthday cake, including all the decorations and at least one of the candles.

For school, Graham had a special, giant-sized lunch box with wheels and a small electric motor to carry all the food that he needed to get him through the day.

One day, Graham's school organised a visit to a local sweet factory.

All the children were very excited at the thought of seeing how sweets were made. And Graham was even more excited at the thought of eating them.

When they reached the factory, the teacher said, "Now, children, stay together and don't wander off on your own."

But Graham wasn't listening. He'd caught sight of something wonderful through a half-open door.

Graham had found a huge store-room, packed from floor to ceiling with delicious sweets of all shapes, colours and sizes.

As he peeked inside, the door slammed shut behind him. Graham was trapped.

"Never mind," he thought. "They're bound to come and look for me. In the meantime, I'll just try a few of these yummy sweets."

Soon it was time to go home. But where was Graham? His teacher realised he was missing and set off to look for him. It wasn't long before he was found...in a large, empty store-room. He had eaten every single one of the sweets and was feeling rather the worse for wear.

Graham had eaten so many sweets that he couldn't walk. He also had a very bad tummy ache and had to go straight home to bed.

"It serves you right, young man," said the doctor. "And I hope it's taught you a lesson."

The doctor told Graham's Mum not to worry.

"He'll soon be better," the doctor said. "And he's promised never to be so greedy again."

"I'm very pleased to hear it," Graham's Mum said, as she offered the doctor a slice of chocolate cake.

Or tried to!

# Look out for the next twelve Little Monsters!

FRIENDLY FRANCO

CLUMSY CLARISSA

BOISTEROUS BILLY

SICKLY SIMON

SERIOUS SADIE

GROWN-UP GABBY

PERFECT PRUDENCE

RUDE ROGER

DANGEROUS DAVE

CURIOUS CALVIN

DIRTY DERMOT

TANTRUM TABITHA

© SPLASH! Holdings Ltd. 1997. 3rd Impression.
Printed in Scotland by Waddies Print Group. Tel: 01506 419393.